JLK

LH

Baby Babka,
the Gorgeous Genius

Baby Babka,
the Gorgeous Genius

by Jane Breskin Zalben

Illustrated by Victoria Chess

Clarion Books • New York

Thanks to Michele Coppola, for seeing the potential; Dinah Stevenson, for pushing me further; Robert Ellinger, executive pastry chef, for sharing his famous babka recipe; and to all younger siblings, of which I am one.

—J. B. Z.

Clarion Books
a Houghton Mifflin Company imprint
215 Park Avenue South, New York, NY 10003
Text copyright © 2004 by Jane Breskin Zalben
Illustrations copyright © 2004 by Victoria Chess

The illustrations were executed in watercolor.
The text was set in 16-point Cochin.

www.houghtonmifflinbooks.com

Printed in Singapore

Library of Congress Cataloging-in-Publication Data

Zalben, Jane Breskin.
Baby Babka, the gorgeous genius / by Jane Breskin Zalben;
illustrated by Victoria Chess. — 1st American ed.
p. cm.
Summary: Unhappy when her baby sister turns out to be a brother, Beryl schemes with her brother Sam to make the newborn disappear, but Uncle Morty helps by telling stories of the love his big sisters had for him, even when he squirted one with pickle juice and ruined another's doll.
ISBN 0-618-23489-6
[1. Babies—Fiction. 2. Brothers and sisters—Fiction. 3. Family life—Fiction.]
I. Chess, Victoria, ill. II. Title.
PZ7.Z254Bab 2004
[E]—dc22   2003027700

ISBN-13: 978-0-618-23489-9
ISBN-10: 0-618-23489-6

TWP 10 9 8 7 6 5 4 3 2 1

CONTENTS

Chapter One

DOUBLE TROUBLE

When Beryl found out the family was going to have a new baby, she nicknamed it "Babka" after her mother's delicious spongy chocolate-crumb cake, hoping the baby would be a little sister as sweet as Mama's prize-winning dessert. *If she is,* thought Beryl, *I am going to love, love, love her.*

"It's time! Now!" Mama cried to Papa, clutching her overnight bag.

"Time for what?" Sam, Beryl's younger brother, was yawning.

"Baby Babka's coming already?" Beryl rubbed her eyes.

Mama nodded yes, and Papa phoned Uncle Morty to ask him to come and stay.

As Beryl and Sam waited for the best uncle in the whole

wide world to appear, they sat at the kitchen table, each with a glass of milk that Papa had warmed for them and a slice of Mama's moist babka.

Then Uncle Morty arrived—in his pajamas—looking rushed and tired. Beryl and Sam's parents were ready to go the hospital. Papa's parting words as he kissed them goodbye were, "Play nice."

Mama leaned over, whispered, "Please don't make a mess for Uncle Morty," and gently dabbed the crumbs off Sam's flushed cheeks.

As soon as they had gone, Beryl repeated those exact

words in her best parent voice, because Sam had climbed onto the fresh sheets in the baby's brand-new crib and said, "I'm going to sleep here."

"Don't touch!" ordered Beryl, staring at the cake crumbs on Sam's fingers.

"I'll touch what I want to!" Sam shouted, winding the musical mobile. "Goo-goo, ga-ga," he wailed loudly as Beryl held her ears.

"Goo-goo, ga-ga to you, you big baby!" cried Beryl. "You're really asking for it," she said, pretending to faint, but peeking out of one eye to see if Sam was watching.

"So are you," Sam said back, crawling out of the crib and plopping onto the thick plush carpet next to her.

They both stared at the moon and stars on the ceiling.

"I wish they were in my room," Beryl said as she dozed off.

Beryl and Sam were sound asleep when Uncle Morty knocked at the door. "Hel-LO? Beryl? Sam? How're my favorite niece and nephew doing?"

They both woke up and said together, innocently, "Fine."

"Guess what?" said Uncle Morty, coming into the baby's room.

"What?" they said at the same time.

"Your father's on the telephone."

Uncle Morty handed them the phone. They listened together as Papa shouted, "It's a boy!"

"Yes! A baby brother! Yippee!" yelled Sam, jumping up and down and spinning in circles like a top. "When can we see him? I'm a big brother now!"

"And *not* the cute baby of the family anymore," Beryl reminded him.

Sam looked stunned for a moment. Then he said, "But at least he's a boy. Just like me."

Beryl's mind was swirling when she finally went to sleep. *Not a girl? No sweet little sister. No ribbons to share. No slumber parties: Girls only.*

Beryl's worst nightmare had come true: *I'm going to be living with two "Sams."*

Two baby brothers. Double trouble.

Chapter Two

THE HOSPITAL VISIT

The next morning, Uncle Morty took Beryl and Sam to the hospital and led them down the hall to "Maternity."

All the babies were lined up in a row in the nursery. All the families were lined up on the other side of the glass window. And almost all the babies and families were squealing.

Papa picked up Sam and put him on his shoulders while Beryl threw her arms around Papa's waist and hugged him.

"Which one is he?" asked Sam. Beryl hoped their baby wasn't one of the loud crying ones.

Papa pointed to the third bassinet from the right in the front row.

"He's got my color hair." Sam proudly stuck out his chest.

"What hair?" whispered Beryl. "He's almost bald, like Uncle Morty."

"Which one is he again?" Sam looked down at Papa, who pointed to a lump tucked in a blue blanket like a baby burrito, gurgling in its sleep.

"My, isn't he gorgeous," said a woman standing next to Papa.

"Why, thank you," said Papa, beaming from ear to ear.

Beryl tugged at Papa's sleeve. "Can we go see Mama now?"

"Only one child at a time. Those are the rules," said a nurse.

"Well, I'm going first," Beryl insisted. She headed down the hall, holding wilted daisies she had picked from their backyard.

Mama's face broke into a wide smile when she saw

Beryl. "For me? Oh, Beryl, they're so-o-o perfect," said Mama.

As Beryl handed her mother the bouquet of flowers, she played with the hospital bracelet on Mama's wrist. The label had Mama's name on it and another name, too.

"It doesn't say 'Babka,'" mumbled Beryl.

Mama stroked Beryl's hair. "Oh, honey, wouldn't that be a silly name for a baby?"

"But Papa sometimes calls me 'Cupcake' or 'Muffin.'

And there's a girl in my class whose name really is Candy.
I thought maybe I could help you pick out a name for
him." Feeling hurt, Beryl held back hot tears and bit her
lower lip.

"Papa named him Zachary—beginning with the letter
'Z'—after his mother, Grandma Zelda." Mama sighed.
"She would have been so happy to see our baby."

Beryl sighed, too, remembering her grandmother.

Mama held Beryl tightly in her arms. Beryl fell into her
hug. She wanted to stay that way a long time, but it was

Sam's turn. As she was leaving, Mama said, "I'll need you to help me with a family party in a week, after Zachary comes home."

What party? Beryl sulked and groaned. *Nobody tells me anything.*

"His name is Zachary," Beryl told Sam as she came out of Mama's room. "Not Babka."

"Great! I'm going to call him Zack," said Sam.

"Zack, another brat," Beryl whispered in Sam's ear.

Zachary is a dumb name, she thought.

A really, really stupid name.

AN OUTING

After the hospital visit was over, Papa stayed with Mama. Uncle Morty took Beryl and Sam home on the bus.

"When I was born," Uncle Morty said, "my favorite uncle came to stay with my sisters—your mama, Aunt Sophie, Aunt Gertie, and Aunt Masha. He took them all to the amusement park at Coney Island."

"Could we go to an amusement park, too?" asked Beryl.

"Sure," agreed Uncle Morty, and off they went.

Uncle Morty bought ride tickets and ice cream cones. They went on the roller coaster. Twice. When they got off, Sam threw up on Beryl.

"Yech!" cried Beryl, carefully wiping splotches off her pink party dress and matching pink shoes.

"I once did that to Aunt Sophie," said Uncle Morty

as he helped Sam clean up. "But she loves me anyway."

"She does?" said a surprised Beryl.

"Uh-huh," said Uncle Morty. "I'm her baby brother."

"Oh," said Beryl, handing Sam a tissue for his sneakers.

Uncle Morty bought them all matching Hawaiian shirts, hot dogs with the works, and iced lemonades. Sam's mustard and sauerkraut splattered Beryl's new shirt, and his hot dog bounced out of the bun onto the pavement.

"Sam! Will you watch out!" Beryl rolled her eyes.

"I once bit into a sour pickle and squirted juice in Aunt Gertie's face. But she loves me anyway," said Uncle Morty.

Beryl giggled, thinking of Aunt Gertie with a face full of pickle juice. She broke her hot dog in half and shared it with Sam.

They rented a rowboat and paddled in a big pond in the park. As Sam leaned over to see the ducks, he splashed water everywhere.

"Sam, you nerd! You nearly tipped the boat over!" Beryl shouted.

"I once dunked Aunt Masha in the Lake in Central Park," said Uncle Morty.

"But she loves you anyway?" said Beryl.

"Uh-huh," said Uncle Morty, grinning. "That she does."

Then they lay in the sun, roasting like three baked potatoes, and stared at the shifting puffy clouds.

"I see a rabbit!" shouted Sam.

"I see it, too!" cried Beryl, tilting her head toward Sam's.

"I have an idea," said Uncle Morty.

He led them to Horatio's Magic Shop on the boardwalk. Inside, it was dark and mysterious. The owner wore a turban.

"When I was little"—Uncle Morty lowered his voice as he picked up a long narrow box with mirrors—"I tried to do the trick where you saw a body in half. I used your mother's favorite doll."

"Uh-oh," Beryl exclaimed. "Did it work?"

Uncle Morty shook his head. "Not exactly."

"Bet she didn't love you *that* day," said Beryl.

"Every so often she still reminds me," said Uncle Morty.

He held an empty large black hat in the air. He turned it around and upside down. Then he put a fancy red silk scarf over it. He tapped the brim of the hat three times with a magic wand. "Ta-da!" he cried, pulling a white rabbit from the hat.

"How did you do that?" Sam screeched.

"A magician never reveals his tricks!" Uncle Morty declared. He smiled mischievously at the owner, who nodded back. Then he put the bunny into the hat, tapped three times, and it was gone.

Uncle Morty bought Sam the large black magic hat and a cape, and Beryl a glittery wand that sparkled and glowed in the dark.

She waved it and leaned toward Sam. "We're going to make Zachary disappear."

Chapter Four

BABY BABKA, THE GORGEOUS GENIUS

When Mama and Papa brought Baby Babka—who was now called Zachary—home, friends and neighbors came to stare. "Gorgeous!" they all squealed, peeking into the crib.

"He's a big, fat, dumb lump," Beryl whispered to Sam.

"He's not as much fun as I thought he would be," admitted Sam.

"I told you so," said Beryl with a sly smile. "What does he do? Nothing."

Beryl overheard Mama telling Uncle Morty, who was staying over for a few days to help, "I think he might be some sort of genius. He's already almost sleeping through the night."

Papa chimed in, "Beryl and Sam were getting us up every two or three hours until they were six months old."

Yeah, right. He wakes us up every night. Beryl yawned. *And during the day all he does is eat and sleep. Some genius.*

While Zachary cooed and made tiny bubbles of saliva, Beryl leaned over to Sam and whispered in his ear, "Babka's gotta disappear. And I mean big-time."

"You think so, Beryl?" Sam said sadly.

"Either he's leaving or I am," insisted Beryl.

Uncle Morty said in Beryl's other ear, "I want to show you something."

He took Beryl and Sam aside and opened his wallet. "These are your baby pictures."

"You keep them in your wallet?" asked Beryl, surprised.

Uncle Morty smiled shyly. "This is you on your first birthday, Sam. You and Zachary have the exact same nose."

"We do?" Sam asked, looking closer.

Uncle Morty nodded yes. "Of course—you're brothers. And here's you, Beryl, without your full set of teeth."

Beryl peered at the photograph and smiled at herself with chocolate babka crumbs all over her chubby cheeks.

"I called you 'The Toothless Wonder of Wantagh.' You and Zachary have the exact same lips."

"We do?" Beryl asked, looking closer.

Uncle Morty nodded yes. "Of course—he's your brother. I always show everyone your baby pictures. You were both gorgeous geniuses, too!"

"We still are!" Beryl insisted. "Well, at least I am." She poked Sam gently.

Uncle Morty sat them both on his lap and handed them a gift. "I got you this new instant camera so you can take pictures and show them to Zack someday. And here's an album for each of you to put them in."

Beryl went over to the bassinet, where Zachary was sleeping. She tickled him under his little chin. Zachary burped in her face.

"Gross," said Beryl, taking a picture.

Sam tried to snuggle Zachary. Zachary burped again. "Super gross!" shouted Sam, who burped along with him. Beryl continued to snap photos, recording every moment.

"When he's older," Sam said, "we'll teach him to belch an entire song. We'll tell him all gorgeous geniuses do that. Right, Beryl?"

"Right," said Beryl, clicking away.

Uncle Morty took a photograph of all three children. He gave Beryl and Sam a sandwich hug and said, "So you can remember the times in your life with Zachary."

Chapter Five

THE FAMILY PARTY

One week later, there was a huge party for the entire family. Beryl and Sam helped Mama put up balloons and streamers. Beryl put out the party cups, paper plates, and pretty napkins. Aunts, uncles, cousins, and friends came from everywhere. There were gifts. Toys. Flowers. And lots and lots of food, with enough babka for everyone. Beryl and Sam felt lost as they sat down in the middle of everybody fussing over the new baby and ignoring them.

Uncle Morty sat down between them on the sofa and said, "I'm going to tell you both a story. One day, long ago, there was a big sister Rose."

"Hey, that's Mama's name!" Beryl piped in, thinking of how much she missed being with Mama, just the two of them alone. And with Papa, too. He told the best stories in the whole world. Even better than Uncle Morty, who told pretty good ones.

"There was your mama—Rose—and three more sisters," continued Uncle Morty, winking at his older sisters.

"Sophie, Gertie, and Masha," added Aunt Sophie as she squeezed onto the sofa next to Uncle Morty.

"And an adorable baby brother named Morton, who was the baby of their family growing up," said Aunt Gertie, pinching Uncle Morty on the cheek.

After finding a little bit of space left at the end of the couch, Aunt Masha added, "Naturally, he was a gorgeous genius."

"It was a given fact. Like the sun in the sky above. His parents showered him with hugs and kisses, and the four sisters nearly squashed him with their love," continued Uncle Morty as if this story had been told many times before.

"Sure they did," the aunts groaned together.

Uncle Morty added, "The baby got so much attention, the sisters put a huge sign on their lemonade stand: FOR SALE. ONE ADORABLE GORGEOUS GENIUS. A NICKLE. TODAY ONLY. LOANS ACCEPTED.

FOR SALE
LEMoNADE 10¢
+ ONE ADORABLE
GORGEOUS geNIUS
A NIKEL. ToDAY ONLY
LOANS   ACCEPTED

Sam broke into the story, out of breath. "Did anyone try to buy you?" he asked Uncle Morty.

Uncle Morty and all the aunts began to laugh.

Beryl answered first. "Silly. He's here, isn't he? And they loved him anyway. Didn't you?" she asked her aunts.

"Yes," said Aunt Sophie. "I held his hand on the first day of school."

"And when she let go, I was okay," interrupted Uncle Morty.

"I taught him how to spell 'antidisestablishmentarianism'

—one of the longest words in the dictionary," said Aunt Gertie.

"I won the spelling bee that year!" Uncle Morty said happily.

"I read bedtime stories to him over and over again until he fell fast asleep," remembered Aunt Masha.

"That's how I became such a good storyteller," added Uncle Morty.

Mama joined her sisters and brother on the edge of the couch. "When I thought he was sleeping, I gave him special butterfly kisses, which tickled his cheeks," said Mama, tickling her brother.

"That's how I became such an expert tickler!" exclaimed Uncle Morty, and he tickled his sister back.

"We decided to keep him. He was kind of cute," said Mama, giggling.

"Was? I still am. It's a given fact," said Uncle Morty.

"Like the sun in the sky above," they all said together.

"The end," said Uncle Morty.

His older sisters laughed.

Everyone else at the party continued to ooh and aah over Zachary.

When it got quiet, while everyone ate dessert — Mama's chocolate babka — Beryl decided it was time for Sam to make the announcement. "The Amazing Beryl!" he said in a booming voice.

He stood on a chair and held up a sheet in front of the wicker bassinet. . . . Beryl tapped her wand three times on the edge. "Abracadabra! Disappear!"

Mama tiptoed behind the sheet, picked up Zachary, and whisked him away.

"My assistant, 'Super Sam,' will take the curtain down," bellowed Beryl. "Drum roll, please!" Papa pounded on an end table.

There was silence in the room. Even Zachary remained hushed. Everyone said, "Wow!" when they saw the empty baby basket.

"Why, he vanished into thin air!" cried out a guest, shocked.

Sam held the sheet back up. Papa did another drum roll. Beryl shouted, "Ta-da!" And *poof!* Zachary reappeared.

"How did you do that?" Papa asked, full of surprise.

Uncle Morty winked at Beryl and she winked back. "A magician never reveals her tricks," she said, and looked over at Mama, who was beaming at her.

Uncle Morty took a picture of the whole family: Beryl with her glitter wand, Sam with his black magic hat and cape, and Mama and Papa holding Zachary.

Beryl wrote the date underneath the photograph, adding: *"Baby Babka the Gorgeous Genius, First Magic Trick."* Then she touched Zachary's lips and turned to Sam. "He *does* look like me. Should we keep him?"

"Of course," said Sam. "He's got my nose."

Just as Mama did to Uncle Morty when he was a baby, Sam leaned over and gave Zachary a special butterfly kiss on his soft pink cheek. And so did Beryl.

She whispered into Zachary's ear, "I will love you anyway. It's a given fact. Like the sun in the sky above."

CHOCOLATE BABKA

This is Mama's prize-winning dessert. Babka means "grandmother's loaf," and the recipe was handed down from Beryl's Grandma Zelda, who brought it over from eastern Europe.

Beryl and Sam like to help Mama make it. Someday, when Zachary gets bigger, he will help, too. Papa always has seconds.

Note: Children shouldn't try making this recipe without a grownup.

Dough

1 package active dry yeast
¼ cup milk, heated to lukewarm
¼ cup unbleached all-purpose flour
2 tablespoons granulated sugar
2 extra-large eggs
1 stick butter, melted and cooled
2 tablespoons sour cream
2 cups unbleached all-purpose flour
Dash of salt

Chocolate-crumb topping

½ cup all-purpose flour
½ cup granulated sugar
2 tablespoons cocoa
1 stick butter, cut into bits

Filling

½ cup granulated sugar
1 tablespoon cinnamon
½ cup chocolate chips
Approximately 3 tablespoons melted butter

Final toppings

Approximately ¾ cup chocolate chips
1-ounce square semisweet chocolate, melted
Powdered (confectioner's) sugar

1. **Dough:** In a small mixing bowl, dissolve yeast in lukewarm milk. Add ¼ cup flour and stir. Let mixture stand 10 minutes or until foamy. Cover with dishtowel. Allow to rest 1 hour at room temperature.
2. In large bowl with electric mixer, blend sugar and eggs, then add melted butter and sour cream. Gradually add 2 cups flour and salt. Knead with dough hook or by hand until soft, elastic dough comes off sides of the bowl. Shape it into a large ball.

3. Place in clean bowl. Cover with a dishtowel. Allow to rise in refrigerator 1 hour.
4. **Chocolate-crumb topping:** In a medium bowl, crumble ingredients between fingers to make "crumbs." **Filling:** Combine cinnamon and sugar in a small bowl. Set both mixtures aside.
5. Butter a 9½-inch tube pan. Preheat oven to 350 degrees.
6. On a flour-dusted surface, roll out chilled dough into as large and thin a rectangle as possible. Brush surface with melted butter.
7. Sprinkle with cinnamon-sugar mixture and ½ cup chocolate chips.
8. Starting with a long side of the rectangle, roll up dough into a long cylinder (like a jellyroll). Place seam side down in prepared pan, forming a circle. Pinch ends together to join.
9. Brush top of cake with additional melted butter. Cover entire top with crumb topping.
10. Bake 45 minutes at 350 until a toothpick inserted in the middle comes out clean.
11. Remove cake from oven to a cooling rack. Dot cake top with chocolate chips and drizzle with melted chocolate. Cool completely before removing from pan. Before serving, lightly dust surface with powdered (confectioner's) sugar.

Yield: 12 servings